Sweet Little Lamb

Written by, Laurie Lynn Holcombe

Archway Publishing books may be ordered through booksellers or by contacting:

Archway Publishing
1663 Liberty Drive
Bloomington, IN 47403
www.archwaypublishing.com
844-669-3957

ISBN: 978-1-6657-1361-0 (sc)
ISBN: 978-1-6657-1362-7 (hc)
ISBN: 978-1-6657-1363-4 (e)

Library of Congress Control Number: 2021920564

Printed in the United States of America.

Archway Publishing rev. date: 11/04/2021

With all the love in my heart, I dedicate this book to my daughter, Tara.

"It's time for sleep my sweet
little lamb."

"Not yet," she said, and
away she ran.

Leap, leap she bounced on her tiny, hoofed feet, she's filled with joy and not ready for sleep.

Across the flower-filled
meadow she trots,

she passes a fawn who still
has his spots.

Climbing up a hill that
is high and steep,

tripping she tumbles
and lands in a heap.

Brushing the grass from
her curly white fleece,
she's landed amongst a
gaggle of geese.

Back on her feet, she is running
quite fast, not certain how long
the sunlight will last.

At the park she watches the children play, they are having fun, but she cannot stay.

Skipping by the pond where
hoppy frogs swim, a wise old
owl hooty-hoots from his limb,

"My sweet little friend you must go home soon.

The sun will set to make room for the moon."

Prancing about as she reaches the farm, she hears a soft sound from inside the barn.

"Goodnight precious lamb, you have had a long day, " moo's Mother Brown Cow, while munching her hay.

Home again, home again,
where it's warm and bright,
the sunny pleasant day has
now become night.

Scrub, scrub in a tub all filled
with bubbles, she washes
away the day of mud puddles.

With a splish, and a splash
she shrieks so loud,

then wraps in a towel soft
as a cloud.

Dance, dance she spins in her pretty pink robe, as if she might twirl across the wide globe.

She brushes her teeth,

then kneels at her bed,

time for her prayers,
she bows down her head.

"As I lay me down to sleep, rainbows dancing at my feet. Angels watch me through the night, and guide me when the sun shines bright.
Amen"

Tucked under covers,
she's ready for sleep, no
more playing for this
sweet little sheep.

Mamma kisses her cheek
and hugs her tight, tells her
she loves her, then turns
out the light.